I0782103

This Book Belongs To The Following Amazing
& Awesome Individual

____

PMA Publishing Group
156 Taunton Avenue # 71
Seekonk, Massachusetts 02771
Copyright 2023

Copyright & Producers Notice

The President Won't is a Registered Trademark with All Rights Reserved
All Rights Reserved. No part of this material in whole or part may be reproduced, transmitted or stored in an information retrieval system in any form or by any means graphic, electronic or mechanical, including photocopying, taping and recording without prior written permission from the author or publisher or producers. All works represent opinion only and should not be relied upon as statements of fact or warrantable or actionable information. This is a work of fiction of author or producers creation and is artificial and fanciful in nature. Names, characters, businesses, places, events, locales and incidents are either products of the authors or producers creation and are meant to be artificial, fanciful, imaginative and or used in a fictitious manner. Any resemblance to actual persons, living or past is not intended to be reliable information. The responsibility for the consequences of your use of any information contained herein lies not with the author ,creator, producer, publisher or distributors of this book. It is advised that all work be reviewed by an individual of legal age before reading or allowing to be read any material contained herein.This book is not intended as medical, health or other advice. If specific services are requested or warranted you are advised to seek a trained professional in your respective area of need or inquiry. All work is designed to promote reading and foster a positive mental attitude in the reader or listener.

For The President Won't Series: All work is meant to be Non-Partisan. No part of any The President Won't Series is meant to support, denigrate or reference any political party as better, more superior, inferior or preferred. All work is designed to encourage a love of history, reading, learning, civic involvement and most importantly foster positive mental attitude.

The President Won't Eat His Vegetables™

By Dylan Thomas Ferreira

A message from The Author

Greetings My Fellow Readers

Thank you for your purchase and promoting literacy and learning. It is my goal to provide you with quality, enjoyable books that you can read independently or with others.

In my work as a teacher, educator, counselor and school psychologist I have found the need for positive, enjoyable reading material that can be both educational and fun.

In addition to attempting to provide a mini-lesson, all books in *The President Won't series* are meant to be non-partisan, humorous and encourage a love of culture, reading, learning, respect for differences and most importantly make you laugh.

I hope you enjoy them.

Please feel free to follow Dylan Thomas Ferreira on Social Media for more information or to find this and other books as they are released.

Sincerely,

Dylan

Mr. Dylan Thomas Ferreira, M.Ed., CAGS, LMHC
National Board Certified Counselor

Not so long ago, there was a President
named President Picky.

President Picky had been doing a good
job and was one of the best Presidents the
country had ever seen.

One day, his family told him:
"Mr. President, you must start eating your vegetables.
They are good for your health!"

But President picky wouldn't listen. "I don't like
vegetables, and I'm the President, so l don't have to
eat them," he said stubbornly.

President Picky loved his burgers, fries, and pizza,
but when it came to vegetables, he simply
refused to eat them.

"Maybe just try a small plate of broccoli,"
said his wife, Ms. Picky.

"*I hate broccoli most of all!*" yelled President
Picky, "Broccoli is like a little tree that tastes
terrible!" he exclaimed. "I'd rather eat the
carpet than eat broccoli!"

At least the carpet has some flavor!" he said.

"Maybe try some carrots", said his wife. "Nope,
I'm Not Gonna Do It," said President Picky,
"Not gonna do it."

As the years went by, President Picky became
known to hate vegetables.

His attitude towards vegetables left him too tired
to do his job or have fun.

He became so tired he needed to take a nap just
to build up enough energy to go to bed.

Then, it was re-election time.

He had a strong opponent who ate his vegetables.

His opponent's name was Bill.

Bill was actually called Burger Bill but always ate his burgers with plenty of healthy veggies.

During the campaign, Burger Bill talked a lot about the importance of eating vegetables, and he even handed out carrot sticks to his supporters. He loved giving handouts, and everyone loved his healthy snacks.

On election day, Burger Bill won the
election by a landslide.

President Picky couldn't believe it.

But then he realized the truth. He had
ignored his health for too long.

And so, with a sad heart, President Picky bid farewell to the White House.

From that day on, President Picky started eating more and more vegetables.

He felt healthy and was more energized than ever before.

And he realized that if he could change, anyone could.

He started to feel so good that he would eat vegetables even if they touched the other foods on his plate.

Then, after the election, Former President Picky
received a gift from President Burger Bill: a little dog

President Picky was delighted with the gift, BUT...
he couldn't believe his ears when he heard the dog's
name was... Broccoli!

"Broccoli?" he asked laughing, "You named my new
dog after the one vegetable I still won't eat."

President Burger Bill smiled and said, "Well, I
figured it was time for you to give broccoli
another chance."

President Picky just rolled his eyes,
he couldn't help but laugh at the idea of a dog
named Broccoli.

As it turned out, having Broccoli around was
just the motivation he needed to start eating
more vegetables and taking regular walks.

Every time he looked at the dog, he was
reminded of the importance of a healthy diet.

Feeling invigorated, President Picky drank two giant carrot and kale smoothies. He then made a speech to all the children in the land, saying:

"Read My Lips, Eat Your Vegetables!

"They may not be as tasty as burgers and fries, but they will make you strong, healthy, and wise!"

And he never forgot the lesson he had learned.

Even the most powerful person in the land needs to eat their vegetables!

After his speech, he walked off the stage.

He quickly found his way to the nearest
bathroom and had a great big poop.

He learned another lesson that day. Eating your
vegetables is really good for your tummy.

From then on, all the children listened to
their wise former president.

They started eating their vegetables, and
they felt better than ever before and had
President Picky to thank.

President Picky and his dog Broccoli
lived happily ever after.

He was always willing to help others and traveled
around the country reminding children to eat healthy.

Every now and then, Ms. Picky would catch the
President sneaking his vegetables to Broccoli.

She usually just laughed since the President was finally
eating his vegetables. Sometimes she reminded him
of what happened when he drank two smoothies and
reminded him not to give the dog too many vegetables.

The End

About the Author

Dylan Thomas Ferreira is not your typical author. As a Licensed
Mental Health Counselor and School Psychologist, he has devoted
his life to the empowerment and well-being of others. With a diverse
career spanning roles as an adjunct professor, educator, teacher,
administrator, and beyond, Dylan has left a profound impact on
countless lives. In every endeavor, he strives to be a versatile and
multifaceted source of positivity and personal growth.